Talia and the RUDE Vegetables

LINDA ELOVITZ MARSHALL • ILLUSTRATED BY FRANCESCA ASSIRELLI

KAR-BEN
PUBLISHING

Text copyright © 2011 by Linda Elovitz Marshall
Illustrations copyright © 2011 byFrancesca Assirelli

KAR-BEN PUBLISHING
A division of Lerner Publishing Group, Inc.
241 First Avenue North
Minneapolis, MN 55401 U.S.A.
1-800-4-Karben

Website address: www.karben.com

Library of Congress Cataloging-in-Publication Data

Marshall, Linda Elovitz.
    Talia and the rude vegetables / by Linda Elovitz Marshall ; illustrated by
Francesca Assirelli.
      p.   cm.
    Summary: City-girl Talia misunderstands her grandmother's request that she
go to the garden for "root vegetables" but manages to find some she thinks are
rude, as well as a good use for the rest she harvests. Includes a recipe for Rude
Vegetable Stew.
    ISBN :978-0-7613-5217-4 (lib. bdg. : alk. paper)
    [1. Vegetables—Fiction. 2. Gardening—Fiction. 3. Judaism—Customs and practices—
Fiction. 4. Rosh ha-Shanah—Fiction.] I. Assirelli, Francesca, ill. II. Title.
PZ7.M35672453Tal 2011
[E—dc22   2010020301

Manufactured in the United States of America
1 - BC - 12/31/10

As she walked toward the garden shed carrying a big pot, Talia puzzled over her grandmother's request.

"Could you go to the garden, please?" Grandma had asked her. "And bring back seven root vegetables: onions, garlic, turnips, parsnips, carrots, potatoes, and rutabagas. Seven is lucky, and with seven root vegetables, raisins, and cinnamon, I'll cook a delicious stew to welcome the New Year."

"Rude vegetables," wondered Talia, "for a sweet New Year?"
She lived in the city and had never done much gardening.

Taking a shovel from the shed,
she walked to the garden.

"Rude vegetables?" she thought again, pushing the shovel into the soil. "How can a vegetable be rude? Does it annoy its brothers and sisters? Does it talk back to its parents?" Talia remembered being bossy to her brother. And she remembered being rude to her parents. "Rosh Hashanah is coming," she thought, "I must ask their forgiveness."

Talia dug up a perfect round onion.
"Beautiful," she thought, "but not what Grandma wants."
She put the perfect round onion aside in a bushel basket .

The next onion she tried to dig would not come out of the ground. She pulled and tugged and tugged and pulled until finally she yanked it free.

"What an ornery onion," she thought. "It won't do what it's told. This must be a rude vegetable."

She put the ornery onion in the pot for grandma. Then Talia went to the garlic patch.

She dug up perfect round garlic bulbs.
"These are gorgeous," she thought, "but not what Grandma wants."
She put the perfect round garlic bulbs in the bushel basket.

Then she dug up an enormous, pinkish purple garlic bulb. "What a garish garlic," she said. "It seems like a big show-off. This must be a rude vegetable."

She put the garish garlic in the pot with the ornery onion and carried the pot to where the carrots grew.

Talia dug up a bunch of long straight carrots.
"Wonderful," she thought, "but not what Grandma wants."
She put the long straight carrots in the bushel basket.
Then she dug up a fat twisted carrot.

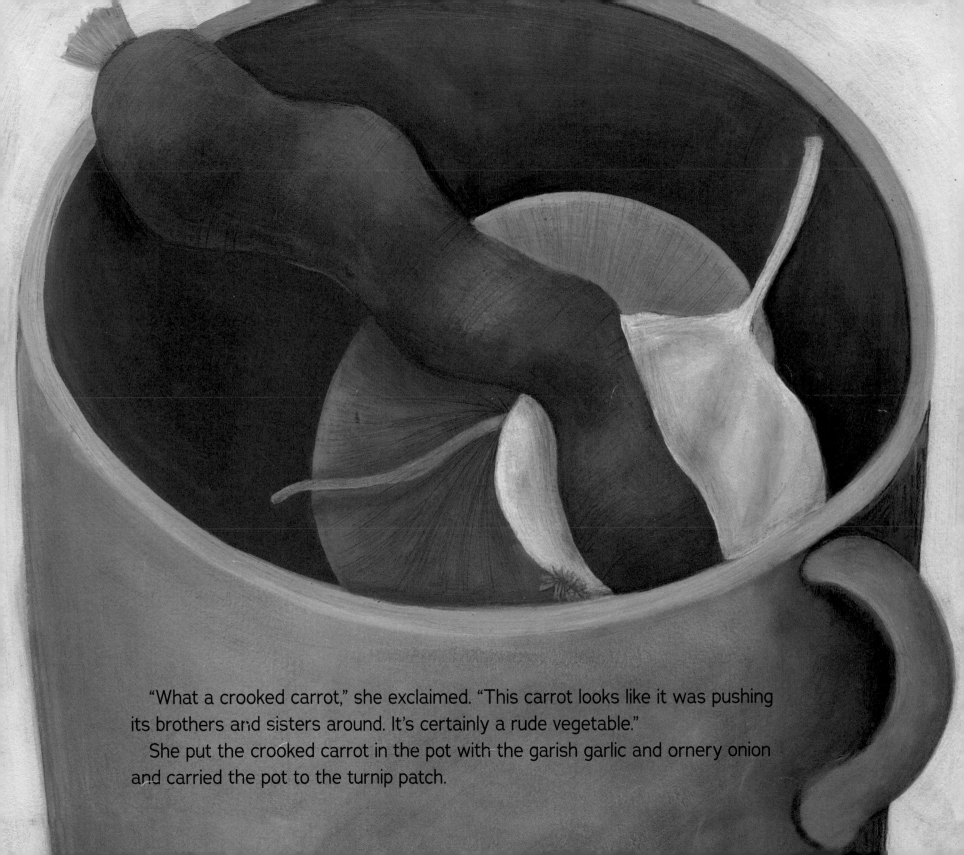

"What a crooked carrot," she exclaimed. "This carrot looks like it was pushing its brothers and sisters around. It's certainly a rude vegetable."

She put the crooked carrot in the pot with the garish garlic and ornery onion and carried the pot to the turnip patch.

Talia dug up four white turnips with pretty purple tops.
"Fabulous," she said, "but not what Grandma wants."
She put the purple and white turnips in the bushel basket.

Talia dug and dug, but the next turnip wouldn't budge.
"This terrible turnip," she thought, "is just what Grandma wants."
Talia pulled and dug and dug and pulled and finally wrenched
the terrible turnip out of the ground.
She put the terrible turnip in the pot with the crooked carrot,
the garish garlic, and the ornery onion.
"Now I have four rude vegetables," she counted,
as she carried the pot to the potato patch.

Talia dug up small round potatoes and lumpy bumpy potatoes. She put the small round potatoes in the big bushel basket. The lumpy, bumpy potatoes went into the pot with the terrible turnip, the crooked carrot, the garish garlic, and the ornery onion.

She carried the pot to the parsnip patch. She dug up long skinny parsnips and put them in the bushel basket. She dug up a big, ugly parsnip with twisted roots.

"This is a peculiar parsnip," she said, and put it in the pot with the lumpy bumpy potatoes, terrible turnip, crooked carrot, garish garlic, and ornery onion.

She carried the pot to the rutabagas and smiled. "Rude-abagas are definitely rude!"
She dug up rutabagas and put them in the pot with the peculiar parsnip, the lumpy bumpy potatoes, terrible turnip, crooked carrot, garish garlic, and ornery onion.

Then she sat down to think. Grandma wanted rude vegetables, but surely someone else could enjoy the others. So she left the pot in the garden and carried the bushel basket to the rabbi.

"Here, Rabbi," she said, handing him the basket. "I've picked enough vegetables for my grandmother. These are extras."

"Thank you, Talia," said the rabbi. "These vegetables will help another family enjoy a sweet New Year."

Talia returned to the garden and took the big pot to her grandmother.
"Grandma," she said. "I've brought you rude vegetables. Just like you wanted."

"Rude vegetables?" Her grandmother laughed.
"They're root vegetables not rude vegetables.
And they're very sweet, just like you. The rabbi called
and told me you gave him food for the hungry.
What a mitzvah!"

"Now," she said, "let's cook the vegetables,
bake some cookies, and get ready for the New Year."
And so they did.

....

"RUDE" VEGETABLE STEW

Can be parve, dairy, or meat depending on ingredients chosen
Preparation Time: Under an hour
Cooking Time: 1-2 hours
Serves a crowd

INGREDIENTS:

The Seven "Rude" (Root) Vegetables:
> *Parsnips – 4- 5*
> *Carrots - 5-6*
> *Turnips - 3-4*
> *Rutabaga – 1 large*
> *Potatoes – 2 large white or sweet*
> *Onion – 1 large or 2 small*
> *Garlic – 1 clove*

Plus . . .
> *Chickpeas – 1-2 cans*
> *Raisins – 2 or more cups*
> *Cinnamon – 2 or more Tbsp.*
> *Cumin– ½ tsp.or more (optional)*
> *Salt and freshly ground black pepper to taste*
> *Liquid – 3 - 4 cups water or broth (vegetable or chicken)*
> *Oil and/or Margarine – 4 Tbsp.*

Peel and cut all the vegetables into chunks. The onion and garlic should be diced. Heat the oil and/or margarine in a large, heavy stockpot and sauté the onion and garlic. Add vegetables and liquid. Cook on medium heat, stirring occasionally so that the vegetables cook thoroughly and do not burn. As the vegetables soften, add the chickpeas, raisins, and spices. Continue to stir occasionally, seasoning to taste. When the vegetables are soft, it's done. This dish may be served as a side dish or, when accompanied by couscous and/or yogurt, an entire meal.